THIS BOOK BELONGS TO

■ ■ ■ ■ ■ ■ ■ ■ ■ ■ ■ ■ ■ ■

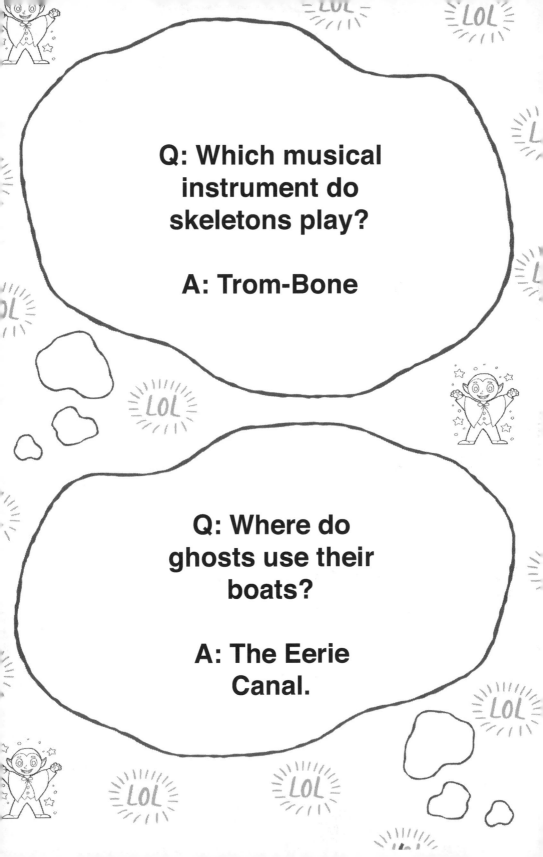

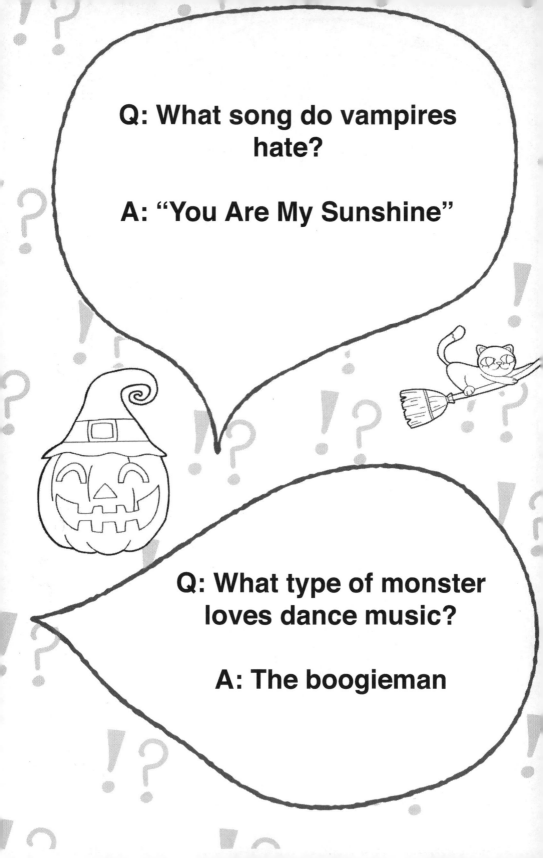

Q: What do skeletons order at restaurants?

A: Spare ribs

Q: What's a ghosts favorite fruit?

A: Booberries.

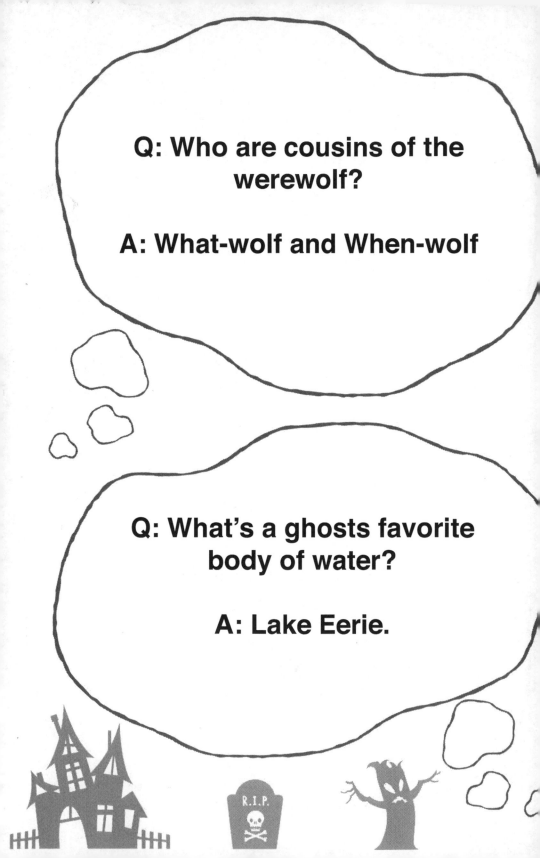

Q: When does a ghost eat breakfast?

A: In the moaning.

Q: What do werewolves read to their children before bed?

A: Hairy tails

Q: What tops off a monster's ice cream sundae?

A: Whipped scream.

Q: What do spirits send their friends while on vacation?

A: Ghostcards

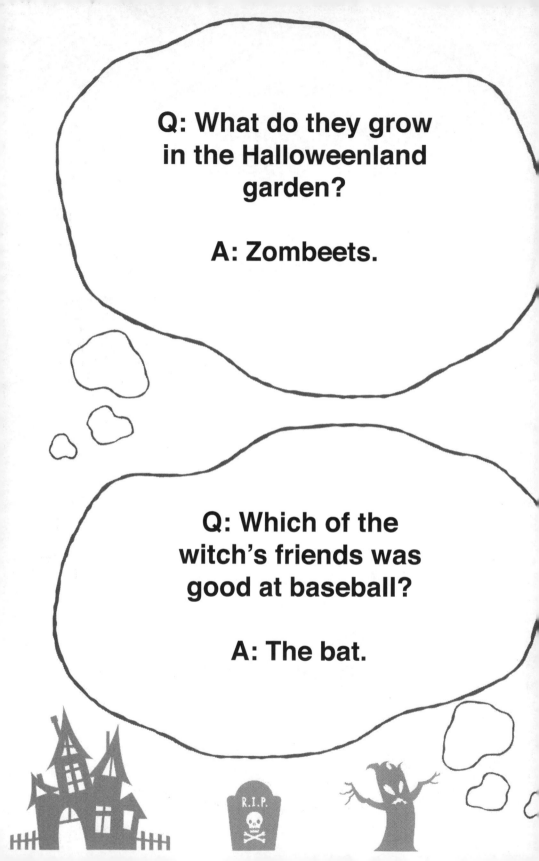

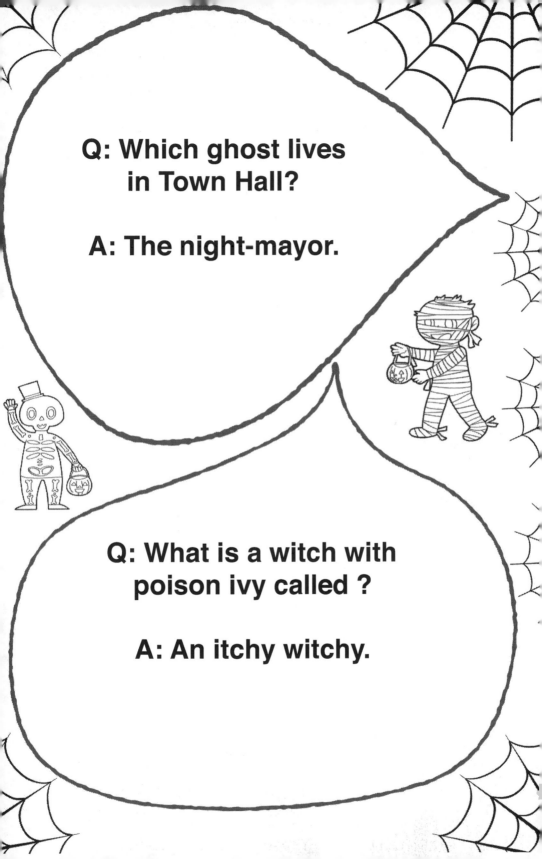

Q: What was the mummy musician's favorite note?

A: The dead sea

Q: Where do ghosts buy their milk and eggs?

A: At the ghost-ery store

Q: What do you call a cold, evil candle?

A: The wicked wick of the north.

Q: Why did the traveling witch throw up?

A: She was broom sick.

Q: When do skeletons laugh?

A: When something tickles their funny bones.

Q: Why did the police officer arrest the ghost?

A: Because he didn't have a haunting license.

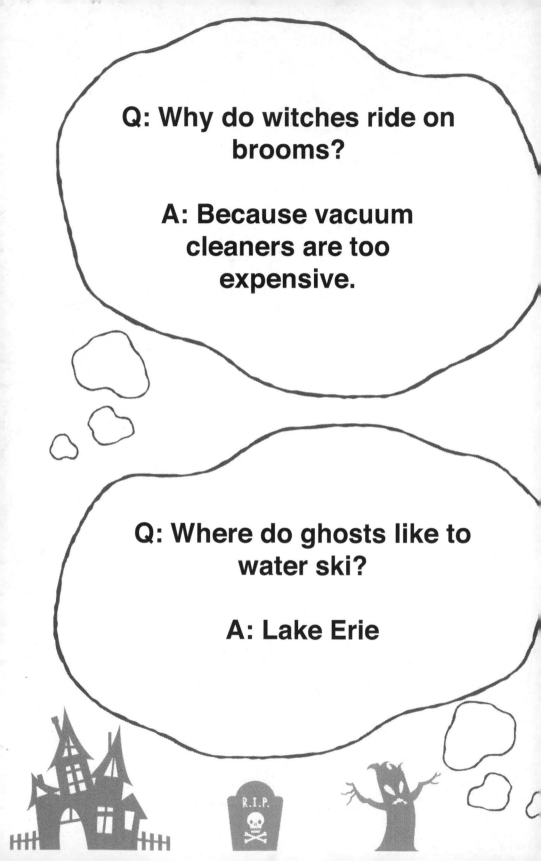

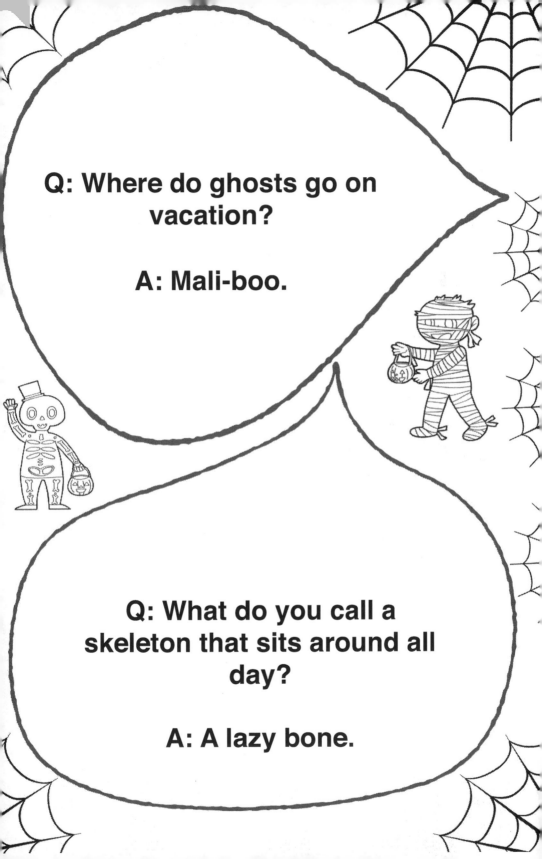

Q: What kind of mistakes do spirits make?

A: Boo-boos

Q: Why was the vampire artist so famous?

A: Because he was great at drawing blood.

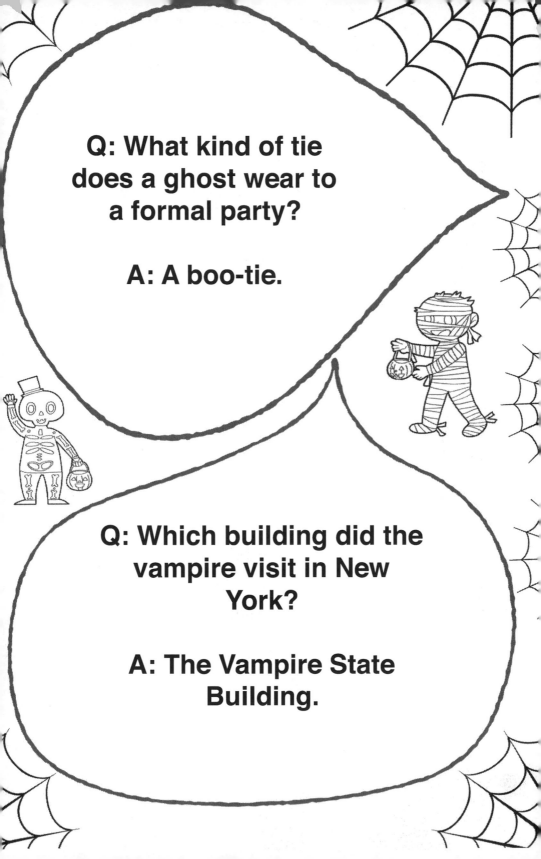

Q: What kind of tie does a ghost wear to a formal party?

A: A boo-tie.

Q: Which building did the vampire visit in New York?

A: The Vampire State Building.

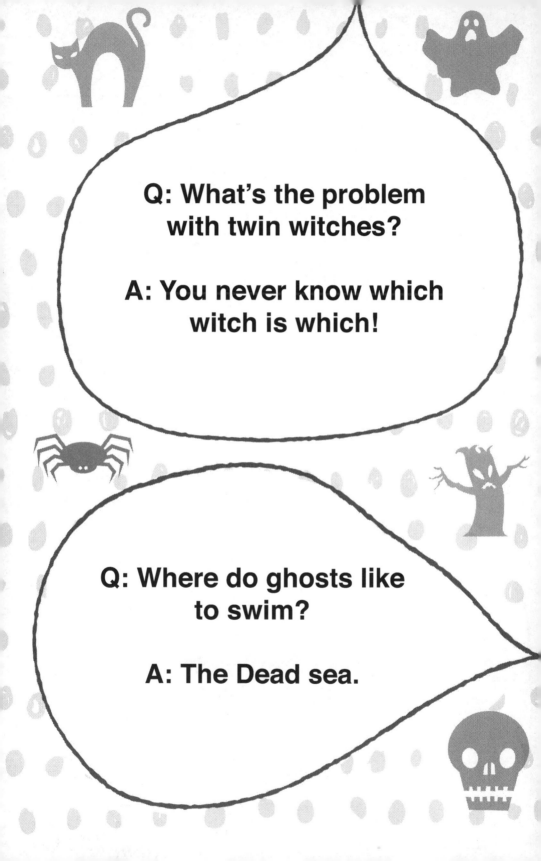

Q: What was the ghosts favorite book?

A: Romeo and Ghouliet

Q: What do you call witches that live together?

A: Broom mates.

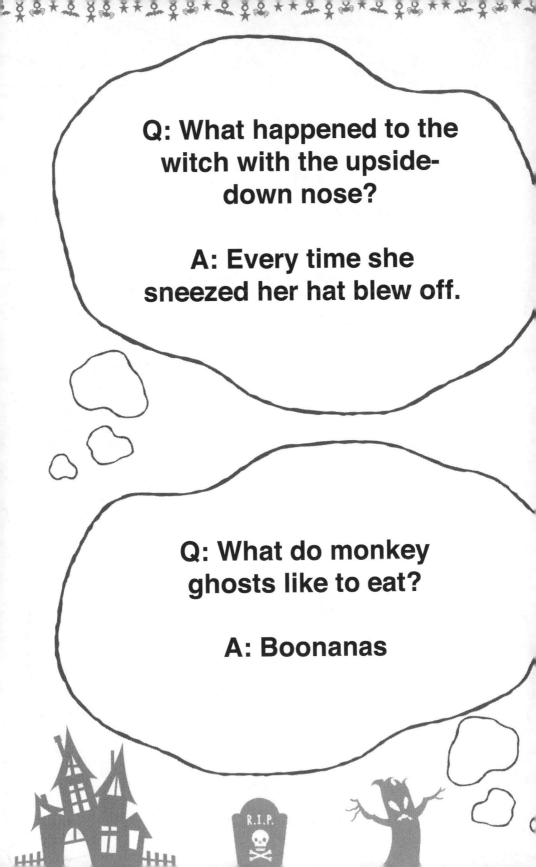

Q: What happened to the witch with the upside-down nose?

A: Every time she sneezed her hat blew off.

Q: What do monkey ghosts like to eat?

A: Boonanas

Q. How does a witch tell the time?

A. With her witch-watch.

Q: What do goblins drink when they're hot and thirsty?

A: Ghoul-aid

Q: What is a monster's favorite snack food?

A: Ghoul scout cookies

Q: What kind of roads do spirits haunt?

A: Dead Ends

Q: Where do baby ghosts stay during the day?

A: Day-scare

Q: Which sport do vampires like to play the most?

A: Bat-minton.

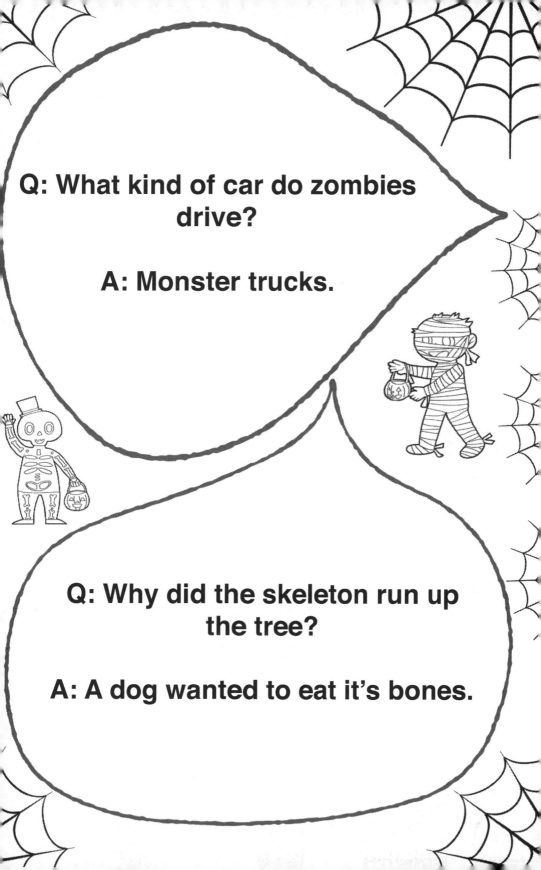

Q: What kind of car do zombies drive?

A: Monster trucks.

Q: Why did the skeleton run up the tree?

A: A dog wanted to eat it's bones.

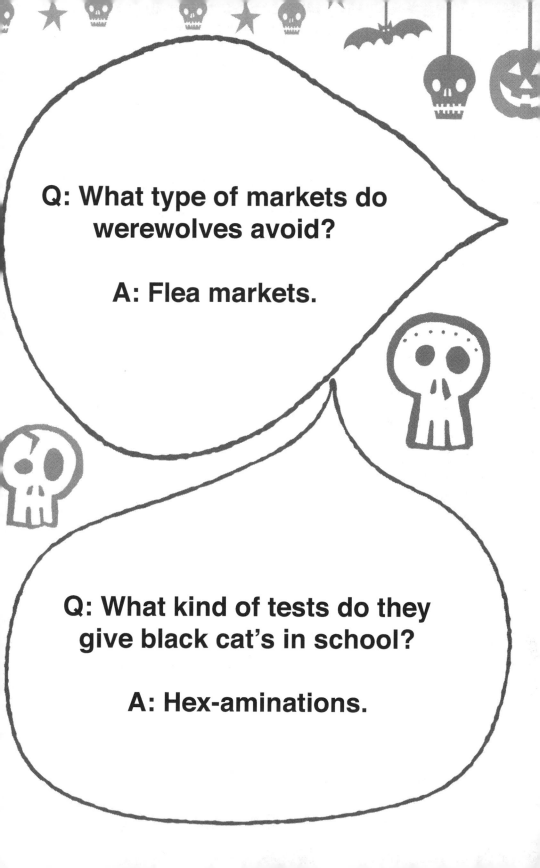

Q: What type of markets do werewolves avoid?

A: Flea markets.

Q: What kind of tests do they give black cat's in school?

A: Hex-aminations.

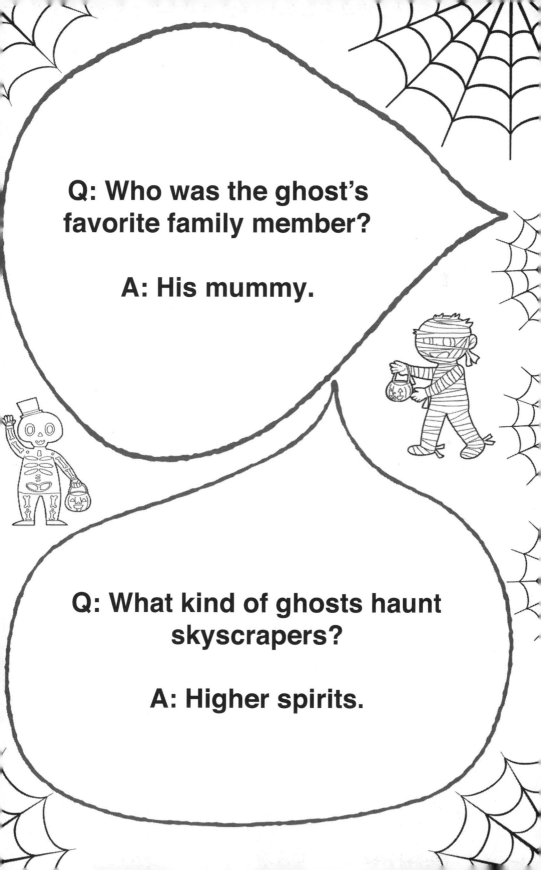

Q: Who was the ghost's favorite family member?

A: His mummy.

Q: What kind of ghosts haunt skyscrapers?

A: Higher spirits.

Q: How can you tell if a mummy has a horrible cold?

A: By his deep, loud coffin.

Q: What kind of music do mummies like most?

A: Wrap music.

Q: Why did a scarecrow win the Nobel prize?

A: He was outstanding in his field.

Q: What was the scarecrow's favorite fruit?

A: Straw-berries.

Q: What is the hardest thing to sell to a ghoul?

A: Life insurance.

Q: Why do ghouls like ice cream?

A: Because it's ghoulilicous.

Q: What's a ghouls favorite bean?

A: Human beans.

Q: What was the ghoul's favorite pet?

A: Ghoulfish.

Q:What monster plays tricks on Halloween?

A:Prank-enstein!

Q:Where does the witch's frog sit?

A:On a toadstool.

Made in the
USA
Middletown, DE